To Nouran, who gives the perfect gifts,
and who is one herself. With love always.
MB

First edition 2020. Library of Congress Catalog Card Number pending. ISBN 978-1-5362-0497-1. This book was typeset in Aunt Mildred. The illustrations were created digitally.
Candlewick Press, 99 Dover Street, Somerville, Massachusetts 02144. www.candlewick.com
Printed in Shenzhen, Guangdong, China. 20 21 22 23 24 25 CCP 10 9 8 7 6 5 4 3 2 1

THE PURPLE PUFFY COAT

Maribeth Boelts

illustrated by Daniel Duncan

CANDLEWICK PRESS

Beetle and Stick Bug walked home from the bus stop, shivering in the cold wind.

"Stick Bug, it's November. That means your birthday is almost here," said Beetle.

"You're right," said Stick Bug. "Just seven more days."

"Well," said Beetle, "I already have your present, because that's just the kind of friend I am. Always thinking of everyone else."

"That's true," said Stick Bug.

"But how can I wait seven days? Your present is SO amazing, and you need it SO much—I must give it to you early," said Beetle.

Beetle scurried inside his apartment, and Stick Bug followed.

Beetle handed Stick Bug a big box.

Stick Bug removed the lid. He stared.

"IT'S A PURPLE PUFFY COAT!" said Beetle. "Isn't it breathtaking?"

"It does look . . . warm," said Stick Bug. "And purple is your favorite color. Thank you, Beetle."

"Try it on! Try it on!" said Beetle.

"You mean now?" said Stick Bug.

"Yes, now!" said Beetle.

Stick Bug encased himself in purple
puffy coat. He looked in the mirror.

"It's showy, isn't it?" said Stick Bug.

"Showy and *glorious!*" gushed Beetle.
"We must strut about."

Beetle and Stick Bug walked the neighborhood.

"Everyone is staring," whispered Stick Bug.

"Did you see they're pointing too?" said Beetle. "They're wondering where they might get a fancy coat like yours. They're wondering if you bought it yourself or if someone generous and thoughtful gave it to you as a gift."

"You're sure?" said Stick Bug.

"I'm sure," said Beetle. "I'll go chat with them."

While Beetle boasted and bragged, Stick Bug waited.

He waited behind a tree,

inside a pile of leaves,

and under a bench.

"Silly Stick Bug," said Beetle. "Come out and be the *center of attention!*"

Stick Bug shuddered.

"I know just what you need," said Beetle. "Every day, we'll have an outing in your purple puffy coat so you can get used to being a spectacle."

Beetle and Stick Bug visited the library,

the grocery store,

and the skate park, with Beetle admiring the purple coat at every turn.

It was the night before Stick Bug's birthday. "I already gave Stick Bug his purple puffy coat," said Beetle. "I'll paint his portrait as another gift."

Beetle sketched and painted.

"I've finished everything but his face," said Beetle. "First, I will try to remember how Stick Bug looks whenever he is wearing his purple puffy coat."

Beetle sketched a huge smile on Stick Bug's face.

"Hmmm," said Beetle. "He doesn't look quite like that."

He sketched a medium-size smile.

"That's not him either," said Beetle.

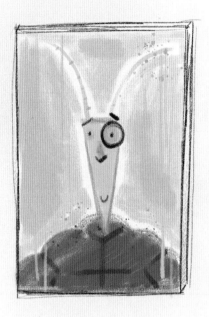

Then he sketched no smile at all.

Beetle stared at Stick Bug's purple puffy . . . *glumness.*

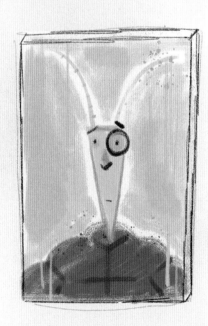

"OH, NO!" wailed Beetle. "That is *exactly* how Stick Bug looks every time he is wearing his purple puffy coat!"

Beetle dashed to the store.

"I'll get Stick Bug a different coat!" he said.

PUFFY COAT BOUTIQUE

Open

PUFFY COAT BOUTIQUE

"A rainbow puffy coat! A sparkly puffy coat!
A polka-dotted puffy coat!"

Then Beetle stopped.

He thought hard about Stick Bug.

Who Stick Bug was—and who he was not.

When the sun came up, Beetle knocked on Stick Bug's door, carrying one teeny-tiny present.

"HAPPY BIRTHDAY, STICK BUG!" shouted Beetle.

"Thank you, Beetle!" said Stick Bug.

"I have something for you," said Beetle.

Stick Bug unwrapped the teeny-tiny box.

He opened the note inside, and read it aloud.

You never need to wear your purple puffy coat ever again.

Your Friend

Beetle x

"Oh, Beetle!" cried Stick Bug. "Are you certain? You love my purple puffy coat!"

"*I* do, but you do not, Stick Bug," said Beetle. "And I want you to be happy."

Stick Bug gave Beetle a hug. "Then you couldn't have given me a better present," he said. "Now, wait here."

Stick Bug opened his wardrobe. He brought out his purple puffy coat.

"I want you to be happy too, Beetle," said Stick Bug. "The purple puffy coat is yours."

"REALLY?" said Beetle.

"Yes, really," said Stick Bug. "Try it on."

Beetle tried it on.

"Too long and too baggy," said Stick Bug.
"I'll fix that right up."

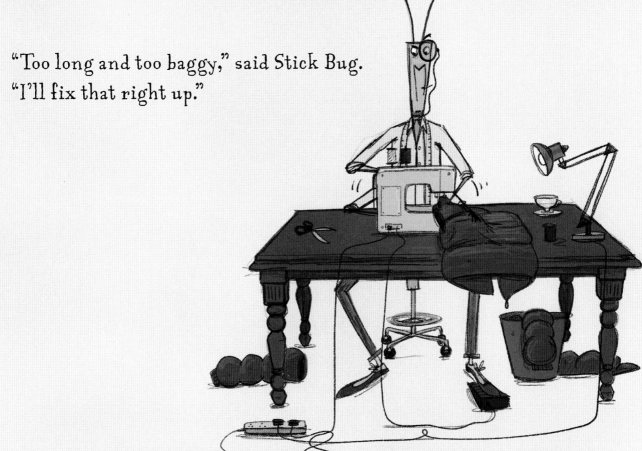

"A purple puffy VEST!" said Beetle. "How do I look, Stick Bug?"

"Magnificent!" said Stick Bug. "And how do I look, Beetle?"

"Like my VERY happy friend on his birthday!" said Beetle.